The Winky Cherry System

OF TEACHING YOUNG CHILDREN TO SEW

My First Patchwork Book HAND & MACHINE SEWING

by Winky Cherry

edited by Linda Wisner and Jeannette Schilling
designed by Linda Wisner

This book belongs to

_____

A letter to Parents, Teachers and Grown-ups:

PATCHWORK, a craft with ancient and modern history, has evolved into a contemporary creative hobby and an American folk art. Patches of fabric are pieced together with seams. Designs have names that provide a record of personal memories and historical events. We continue to reproduce and rearrange these fabric blocks with a sense of satisfaction that can only be described by doing it.

I have been teaching boys and girls sewing skills, and, as a result, life skills, for almost 20 years. *My First Patchwork Book*, the FIFTH LEVEL in **The Winky Cherry System of Teaching Your Children to Sew**™ series, introduces the process of patchwork to beginners as they make a FOUR PATCH BLOCK by hand or machine. The sequence of construction is as important as the finished work. This book introduces the iron as a sewing tool, and teaches a beginner to use a SEAM GUIDE. Young beginners will sew this project with a ½" seam allowance. When children understand elementary patchwork math and can make an accurate ½" measurement consistently, they are ready to use a traditional ¼" patchwork seam allowance.

The first part of patchwork is GETTING READY to sew by choosing the project, getting supplies, preparing the fabric and using a template with a seam allowance to make fabric patches. STITCHING and PRESSING is the second part. Checklists for stitching seams help the child remember to make consistent seam allowances and to match seams that cross. The third part of patchwork is PRACTICING to improve skills.

ALPHABET CODE FLAGS provide a simple patchwork block for each letter of the alphabet to make into pillows or flags, or save to make a quilt.

My First Quilt Book, the next in this series, uses nine 10" patchwork blocks to make a quilt. Sewing classes can be built around each of the books in this series. I have developed teaching information, which is available from Palmer/Pletsch at (503) 274-0687.

Winky Cherry

Winky Cherry

Copyright © 1997 by Palmer/Pletsch Publishing

Illustrations by Jeannette Schilling and Kate Pryka

Library of Congress Catalog Card Number
Published by Palmer/Pletsch Publishing
P.O. Box 12046, Portland, OR 97212-0046
Printed by Your Town Press, Salem, Oregon, USA

ISBN 0-935278-48-6

Once upon a time a child like you made a PATCHWORK BLOCK and this is how!
Would you like to make one now?

PATCHWORK is a creative and practical way to sew.

Small PATCHES of fabric are PIECED together with SEAMS to make a BLOCK of PATCHWORK.

Four Patch Block

PATCHWORK BLOCKS HAVE NAMES

Many PATCHWORK BLOCKS were named by people who made them a long time ago.

Simple names come from the design of shapes and colors inside the BLOCKS you sew.

Some BLOCk names tell stories of life, nature, religion, history, common things and places.

PATCHWORK made from fabric PATCHES holds memories, from a wedding dress or outgrown clothes, of special times and faces.

Betsy Ross's American flag was PIECED with stripes.

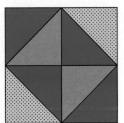

Broken Dishes

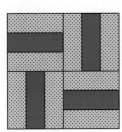

Roman Stripe

Double Four Patch

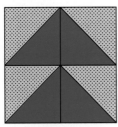

Wildgoose Chase

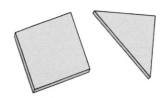

A **TEMPLATE** is a pattern for a PATCH in a BLOCK. It is made of plastic or poster board.

The first PATCHWORK TEMPLATES were made of wood or tin.

RULES FOR PATCHWORK

1. MAKE SMALL PROJECTS WITH BIG PIECES FIRST. Setting limits helps you to finish what you start and learn something new.

2. USE SHAPES with SQUARE CORNERS and STRAIGHT LINES. Make edges and cross seams match on simple shapes first.

3. WORK ON A FLAT SPACE. Make sure it is clean and neat so you can lay the pieces flat.

4. USE RECOMMENDED SUPPLIES. Buy 100% woven cotton fabric for PATCHWORK projects. Read the labels on the fabric bolts.

5. USE AN IRON TO PRESS FABRIC FLAT BEFORE TRACING PATCHWORK SHAPES ON FABRIC.

6. USE a PERFECT TEMPLATE to mark and cut PERFECT FABRIC PATCHES.

7. PLACE the OUTSIDE EDGE of a PERFECT TEMPLATE along a STRAIGHT THREAD LINE when marking pieces for PATCHWORK design.

8. USE A SEAM GUIDE to make ALL of the SEAM ALLOWANCES THE SAME SIZE. Measure and stitch accurately.

9. USE AN IRON TO PRESS PATCHWORK SEAM ALLOWANCES in one direction, usually toward the darker fabric.

10. FIX MISTAKES. Undo and restitch seams with tiny tucks or that do not match at cross seams.

11. USE A CHECKLIST TO SEW. A list helps you remember what to do.

12. FINISH YOUR WORK. Do not begin something new until you complete what you started to do.

THINGS YOU WILL NEED:

☐ **6" template** comes in book kit or to make one see page 40

☐ **alphabet block patterns** (see page 32)

☐ **pincushion** with strawberry to sharpen the needle

☐ **pencil**   ☐ **straight pins**

☐ **needle**   ☐ **special pin**

☐ **thread** mercerized cotton thread

☐ **scissors** for cutting fabric AND another pair for cutting paper or poster board

☐ **snippers** for cutting THREAD

☐ **iron**

☐ **ironing board**

☐ **sandpaper #5**

☐ **woven 100% cotton fabrics**

- two to four prints for Four Patch Block (page 8)
- red, blue, yellow, white and black solids for the alphabet code flags (page 29)

You may also ask your local quilt store's clerks to recommend their favorite quilting tools.

A 6" poster board template for the Four Patch Block is included in the kit,

OR

trace this shape onto template plastic or poster board (see page 40).

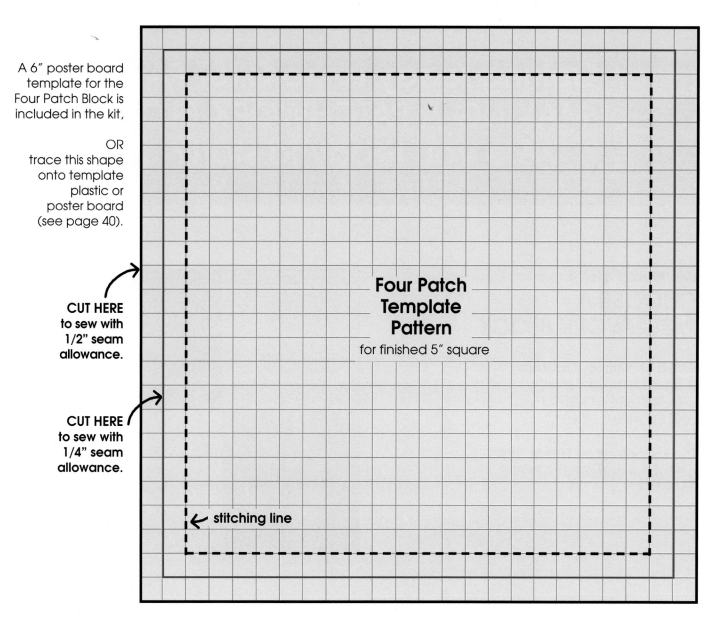

CUT HERE
to sew with
1/2" seam
allowance.

CUT HERE
to sew with
1/4" seam
allowance.

**Four Patch
Template
Pattern**
for finished 5" square

← stitching line

OPTIONAL:

❏ **sewing machine** for machine stitching

❏ **masking tape** as a sewing machine seam guide

❏ **polyester fiberfill** for pillow stuffing

❏ **spray starch** to stabilize fabric (page 34)

❏ **3/8" dowels** for flags

❏ **template plastic or poster board**

❏ **T-square** 12"-long for template making

❏ **quilter's ruler** thick, gridded clear acrylic

❏ **transfer web** for template making

Getting ready is the FIRST PART of MAKING A PATCHWORK BLOCK. Are you ready to start?

GET READY STEP 1

CHOOSE A PATCHWORK BLOCK

A BLOCK with four squares is an easy-to-sew design with SQUARE CORNERS and STRAIGHT LINES.

The shapes inside THIS BLOCK give it the name FOUR PATCH.

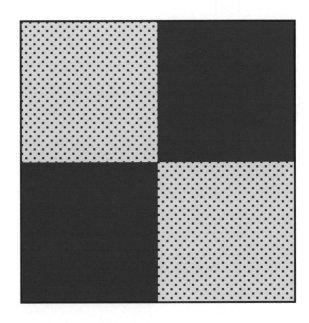

PATCHWORK MATH IS MEASURING AND PLANNING
the size of the BLOCK,
the size of the PIECES,
and the size of the SEAM ALLOWANCE.

PLAN THE SIZE OF THE BLOCK

THE SIZE OF A FINISHED PROJECT DOES NOT INCLUDE SEAM ALLOWANCES.

A 6" fabric square
sewn with a 1/2" seam allowance
will make a 5" FINISHED PATCH.

Four 6" fabric squares
sewn with a 1/2" seam allowance
will make a 10" FINISHED
FOUR PATCH BLOCK.

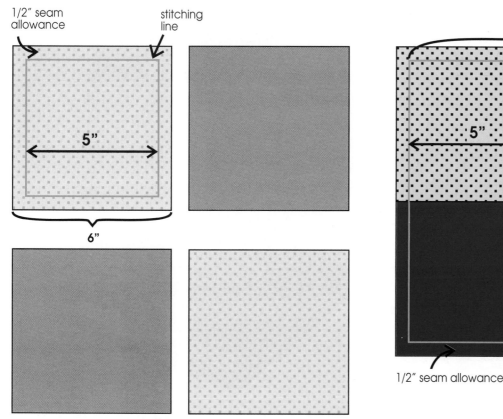

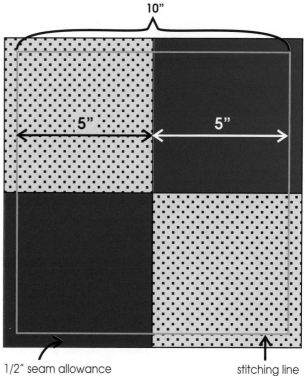

A SEAM ALLOWANCE is the space between the stitching and the edge of the fabric.
Patchwork is commonly sewn using 1/4" seam allowances.
This book shows 1/2" seam allowances that are easier for young beginners to sew.

CHOOSE THE FABRIC

USE **100% WOVEN COTTON** FABRIC.

Choose four
different fabrics OR...choose two.

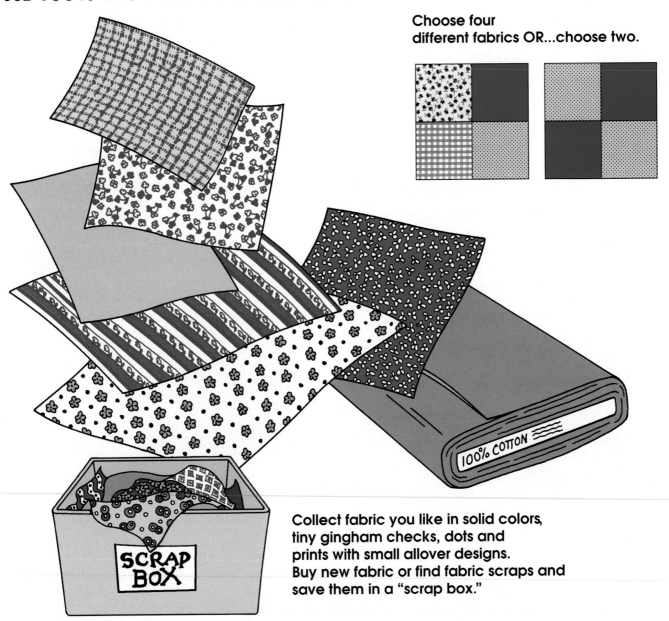

Collect fabric you like in solid colors,
tiny gingham checks, dots and
prints with small allover designs.
Buy new fabric or find fabric scraps and
save them in a "scrap box."

GET READY STEP 4
PREPARE THE FABRIC

WASH AND DRY THE FABRIC.

Learning to WASH and DRY fabric
is PART OF LEARNING TO SEW.
IF SOMEONE DOES IT FOR YOU
YOU WON'T LEARN WHAT TO DO.

Washing fabric before you sew
is important because
some fabrics BLEED (lose color)
or SHRINK (get smaller)
when they get wet.

Mr. Tuck and Ms. Wrinkle
will help to remind you
to be careful not to make
boo-boos.

11

USE AN IRON TO PRESS THE FABRIC

AN IRON IS A TOOL WITH SAFETY RULES.

Plug in the IRON before you use it,
and unplug it when you are through.
FOLLOW THE RULES for using an IRON
and be careful when you do.

TEST THE TEMPERATURE.

READ the HEAT CONTROL
on the IRON to find the
temperature setting
for the fabric you are using.

SET the dial
for COTTON FABRIC.

CHECK TO SEE
IF THE IRON IS HOT.
Press the IRON
to the ironing board.
Stand the iron on its heel
and feel the spot.

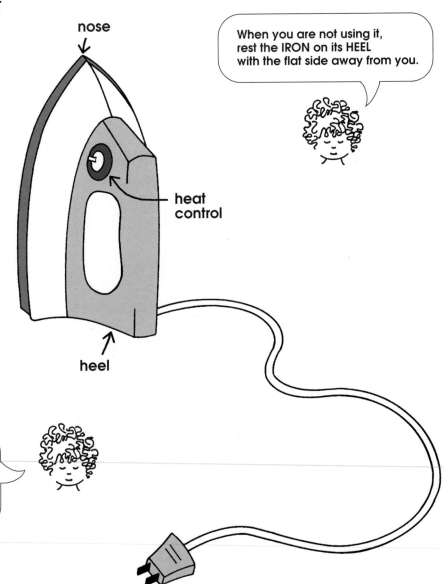

nose

heat
control

heel

When you are not using it,
rest the IRON on its HEEL
with the flat side away from you.

If the IRON is too hot
it can burn the fabric.
If the IRON is too cool
it won't press out the wrinkles
to make the fabric FLAT.

IRON THE FABRIC TO MAKE IT FLAT

Keep the RIGHT SIDE of the fabric fresh and new.
The IRON can burn, shine or dull fabric, if you're not careful what you do.

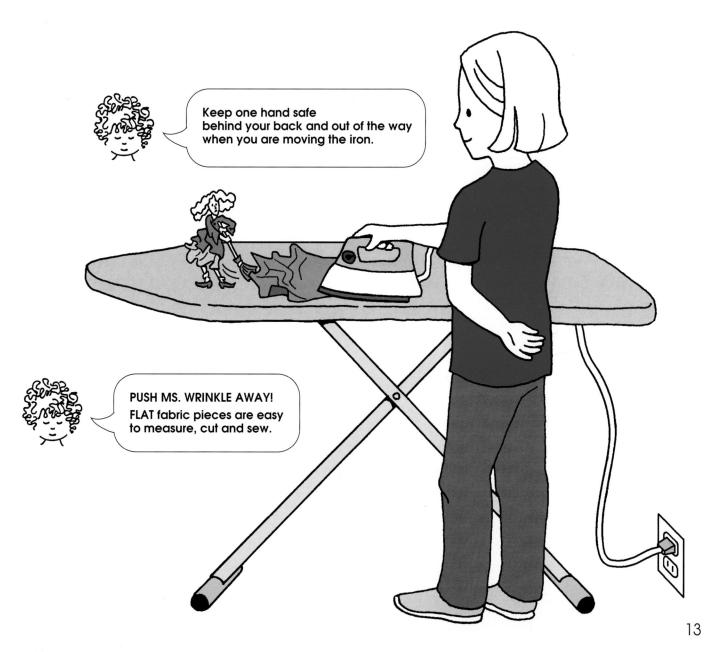

Keep one hand safe
behind your back and out of the way
when you are moving the iron.

PUSH MS. WRINKLE AWAY!
FLAT fabric pieces are easy
to measure, cut and sew.

13

USE A TEMPLATE TO DRAW FOUR SQUARES ON FABRIC

PLACE THE TEMPLATE.

On the **WRONG SIDE** of the fabric place a **STRAIGHT EDGE** of the **TEMPLATE** along a **STRAIGHT THREAD** in the woven fabric.

Tape **SANDPAPER** to the table rough side up under the fabric to keep the fabric from moving when you draw.

DRAW AROUND THE TEMPLATE.

Use a pencil to draw around the edges of the template to mark the **CUTTING LINE**.

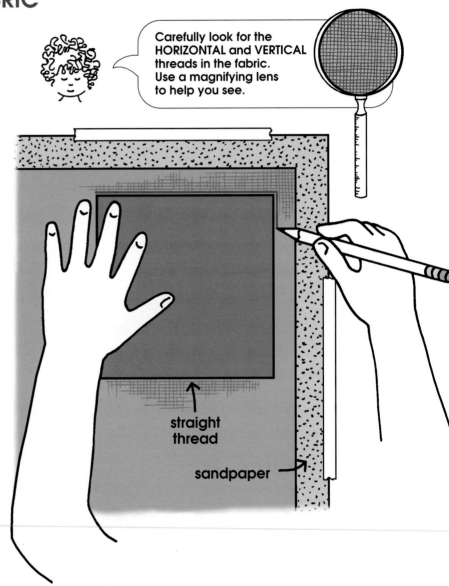

Carefully look for the **HORIZONTAL** and **VERTICAL** threads in the fabric. Use a magnifying lens to help you see.

straight thread

sandpaper

CUT THE FABRIC PATCHES

Cut carefully along each pencil line.

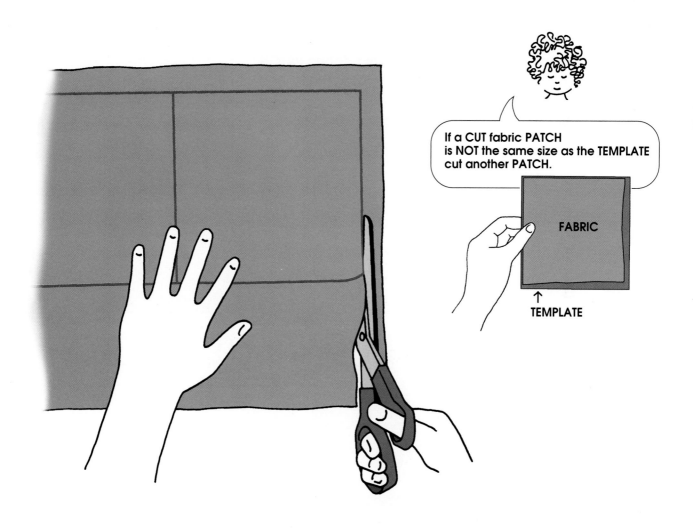

If a CUT fabric PATCH
is NOT the same size as the TEMPLATE
cut another PATCH.

FABRIC

↑
TEMPLATE

LAY OUT THE BLOCK

PLACE THE FOUR CUT PATCHES TO LOOK LIKE THE FOUR PATCH BLOCK.

Put the four fabric PATCHES RIGHT SIDE UP to see
where you want each PATCH in the BLOCK to be.

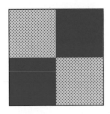

NUMBER THE PATCHES

Write a number in pencil on the back of each fabric PATCH
to show how to place them when you sew them together
to make the FOUR PATCH block.

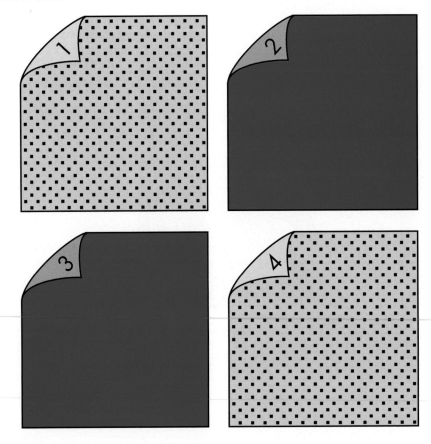

ROW #1

ROW #2

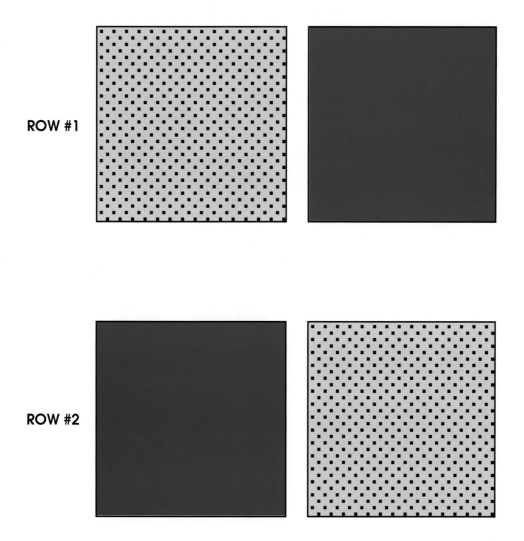

FLIP PATCH #2 ONTO PATCH #1

**Pick up PATCH #2, TURN IT OVER,
and PLACE the RIGHT SIDE DOWN on top of PATCH #1.**

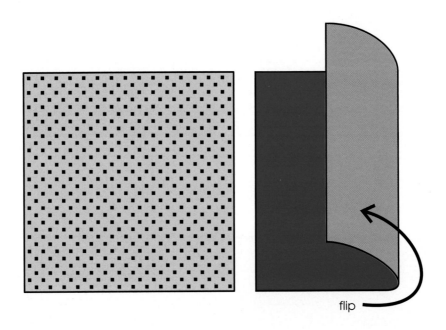

flip

DRAW A SEAM GUIDE LINE ON THE FABRIC

PIN THE PATCHES TOGETHER

A seam guide helps you make all the seam allowances the same size.

MATCH the edges of the fabric carefully and place pin points out and pin heads in.

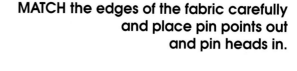

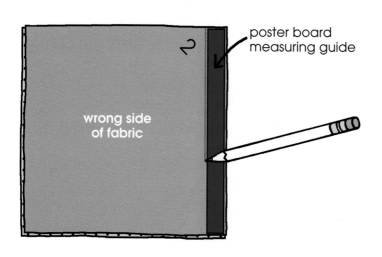

poster board measuring guide

wrong side of fabric

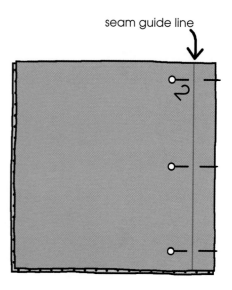

seam guide line

MAKE A MEASURING GUIDE.

Use a ruler, a pencil and scissors to make a strip of poster board or template plastic, as long as the block and the width of your seam allowance.

STITCHING and PRESSING is the SECOND PART OF MAKING A PATCHWORK BLOCK.

TO STITCH BY HAND

GET A NEEDLE AND THREAD READY TO SEW.

Thread the needle, pull the threads even and make a knot.

USE RUNNING STITCHES.

Make down and up stitches 1/8" apart on the LINE.

The KNOT on the end of the thread locks the stitches.
At the end of the seam remember to LOCK the stitches, too.

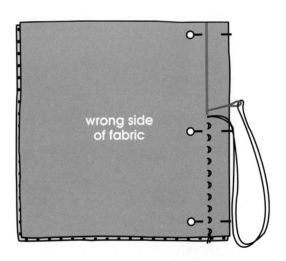

wrong side
of fabric

My First Sewing Book taught you to make
SAVE THE LOOP LOCK STITCHES.
If you don't remember
go back and take a look.

If you are sewing by hand skip the next page.

PLACE SEAM GUIDE TAPE ON THE MACHINE.

A PIECE of MASKING TAPE 1/2" from the NEEDLE measures the 1/2" SEAM ALLOWANCE space between the stitches and the matched edges.

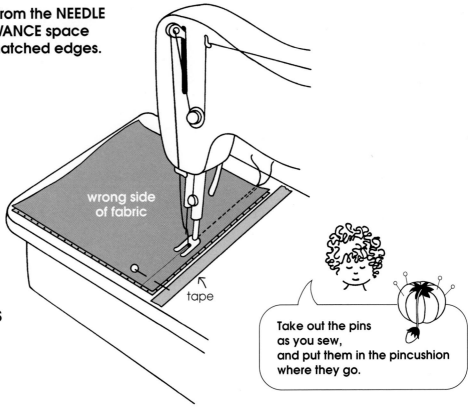

wrong side of fabric

tape

STITCH THE SEAM.

Set the machine to sew eight to ten stitches per inch.

Put the pinned squares under the NEEDLE with the PINS POINTING TO THE TAPE.

Guide the MATCHED EDGES along the TAPE and go slow to make all SEAM ALLOWANCES the same size as you sew.

Take out the pins as you sew, and put them in the pincushion where they go.

BACK TACK to LOCK the stitches at the beginning and the end of the seam using the REVERSE CONTROL on the machine.

SNIP the long, dangly leftover threads when done.

PRESS THE SEAM ALLOWANCE

Place the stitched fabric PATCHES
on the ironing board
with the darkest fabric on top.

Press to SET THE STITCHES.

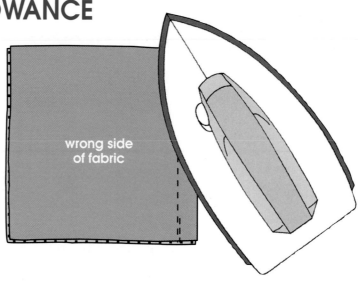

PRESS FLAT carefully.
Ms. Wrinkle likes to make
the fabric look wrinkly!

Mr. Tuck likes to make folds in the fabric
when you press or stitch.
These are sewing problems
that YOU must fix!

Flip the darker PATCH over to lay flat on the ironing board
and use the iron to PRESS the PATCHES
and SEAM ALLOWANCES FLAT.

The SEAM ALLOWANCES will be under the darker side.

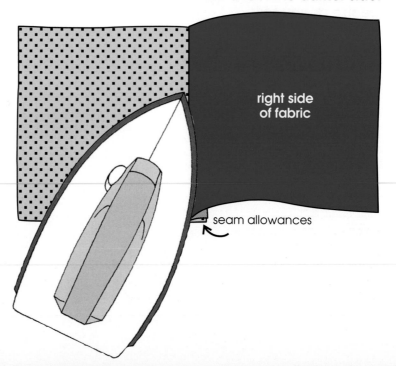

Use a CHECKLIST to remind you what to do.

STITCHING CHECKLIST

☑ **LAY OUT pieces in rows, RIGHT SIDE UP.**
Make two rows with two patches in each row.

☑ **Get ready to stitch.**
1. PUT RIGHT SIDES of two PATCHES TOGETHER.
2. Mark SEAM LINES on wrong side of fabric.
3. MATCH EDGES.
4. PIN. Place pin points out and heads in.

☑ **SEW the seam.**
1. USE A SEAM GUIDE to make all the SEAM ALLOWANCES the same size.
2. BACK TACK to LOCK the stitches at the beginning and the end of the SEAM.
3. CHECK the front and the back of the seam for wrinkles and tucks. If there are any tucks, undo the stitches, press the patches, and sew them together again.

☑ **PRESS the SEAM.**
1. PRESS along the stitching line to SET THE STITCHES.
2. PRESS the darker patch away from the lighter one on the right side of the fabric.
3. CHECK the front and back of the SEAM for wrinkles and tucks.

LAY OUT ROW #1 AND ROW #2, RIGHT SIDES UP

Place the rows so the seams line up
and the two patches of the same fabric
are not next to each other.

Find SEAMS that CROSS
on the clothes you wear.
Look at the SEAMS
  under your arms.
Do you see CROSS SEAMS there?

FLIP, MATCH EDGES, AND PIN THE LONG SEAM

PLACE ONE **SPECIAL PIN** TO HOLD THE CROSS SEAMS MATCHED.

YOU decide what pin will be YOUR SPECIAL PIN.
It will remind you to do something new.
This pin STAYS IN when the stitches go through.

Flip ROW #1 onto ROW #2
RIGHT SIDES TOGETHER,
and **MATCH THE EDGES.**

Poke a SPECIAL PIN
DOWN THROUGH THE STITCHES
on ROW #1 and ROW #2
to HOLD the cross seams matched.

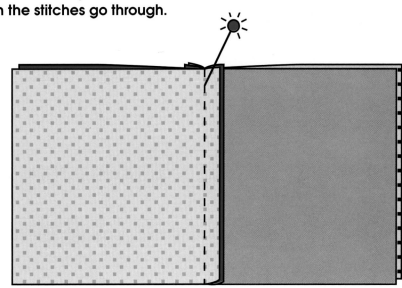

Place two pins
to hold the SEAM ALLOWANCES
and more pins to keep the
long edges matched.

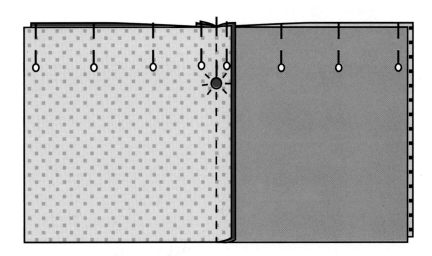

STITCH THE SEAM

PUT THE PINNED ROW UNDER THE NEEDLE WITH PINS POINTING TO THE TAPE.

BACK TACK to LOCK the stitches as you start to sew.
Remember to take the REGULAR PINS out as you go.

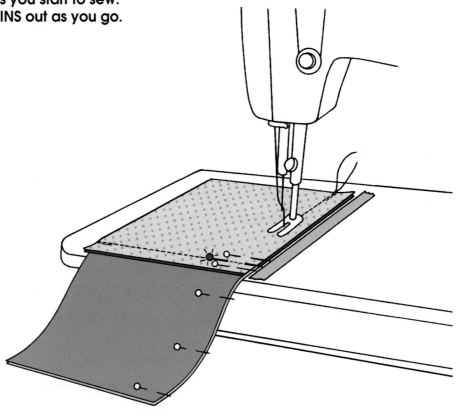

USE YOUR HAND
TO TURN THE WHEEL,
TO WALK THE NEEDLE
OVER THE SPECIAL PIN.

The SPECIAL PIN reminds you
to LEAVE IT IN,
to keep the CROSS SEAMS
    MATCHED
when stitching.

REMEMBER to LOCK the stitches
at the END of the SEAM too,
and put pins away.

CHECK to see if the CROSS SEAMS MATCH
and the SEAM ALLOWANCE
   is stitched accurately.
Undo a boo-boo
and REDO the stitches carefully.

TUCKS and UNMATCHED SEAMS
are lessons for you.
Learn from mistakes.
What did you do?

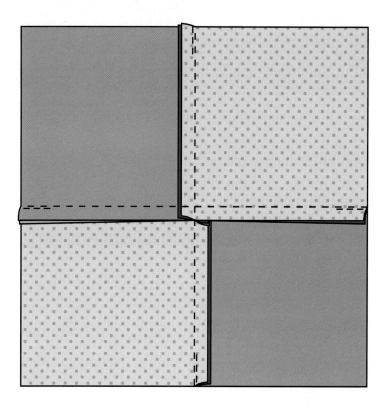

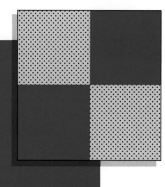

Your first PATCHWORK BLOCK is done.
Do you want to make another one?

To use the BLOCK to make
a PILLOW or a FLAG, turn the page now.

THE THIRD PART OF PATCHWORK IS FINISHING THE BLOCK AS A PILLOW, A FLAG OR AS PART OF A QUILT.

1. Cut a BACK for the pillow.
2. Pin the BLOCK and the back right sides together.
3. Use a seam guide as you stitch around all sides, leaving an opening for turning.
4. Trim the corner points.

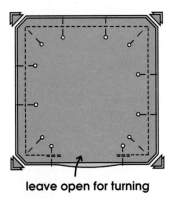

leave open for turning

5. Turn right side out and poke out corner points.

6. Stuff the pillow.

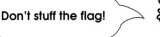
Don't stuff the flag!

7. Fold the SEAM ALLOWANCE in along the open edge and pin.
8. Overstitch and lockstitch by hand.

TO MAKE A FLAG:

After turning, use a 1/2" seam guide to stitch a seam along the left side of the BLOCK.

Take out the stitches at the bottom to open a hole for a 3/8" wooden dowel flag pole.

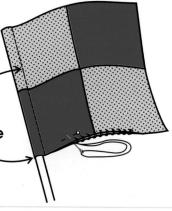

A PALMER/PLETSCH BOOK FOR CHILDREN

My First Quilt Book MACHINE SEWING

by Winky Cherry

FOR AGES 7 AND UP

YOU MAY ALSO USE PATCHWORK BLOCKS TO MAKE A QUILT.

My First Quilt Book will show you how. You can learn something new!

A PATCHWORK BLOCK ALPHABET

is a code sailors, soldiers, pilots and astronauts use.

Each FLAG has a CODE NAME,
an IMPORTANT MESSAGE
and a LETTER NAME to use with other flags
to write words.

THE PLACEMENT OF SHAPES AND COLOR GIVE A BLOCK A NAME.

When the shapes in two blocks
are the same, like "H" and "K,"
THE USE OF COLOR
GIVES EACH BLOCK A
DIFFERENT NAME.

"H"

"K"

To make CODE FLAGS, follow the colors
in the photo on the inside back cover
or follow the code below.

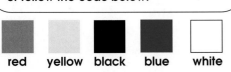

red   yellow   black   blue   white

The MORSE CODE
is an alphabet of dots (**.**)
and dashes (**—**).

A · —
ALPHA

DIVER BELOW. KEEP WELL
CLEAR AT LOW SPEED. (Stay
away from me and go slowly.)

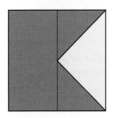

B — · · ·
BRAVO

I AM CARRYING DANGEROUS
GOODS. (The things I have on
my boat are not safe.)

C — · — ·
CHARLIE

YES!

D — · ·
DELTA

KEEP CLEAR OF ME.
I AM MOVING WITH
DIFFICULTY.

E ·
ECHO
I AM ALTERING MY COURSE
TO STARBOARD.
(I'm moving to the right.)

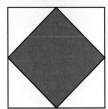

F · · – ·
FOXTROT
I AM DISABLED. COMMUNICATE
WITH ME.
(I cannot move. Talk to me.)

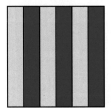

G – – ·
GOLF
I NEED A GUIDE.

H · · · ·
HOTEL
I HAVE A PILOT ON BOARD.
(I have a guide on my boat to
help me go where I want to go.)

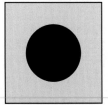

I · ·
INDIA
I AM ALTERING MY COURSE
TO PORT.
(I am moving to the left.)

J · – – –
JULIET
I AM ON FIRE; KEEP CLEAR
OF ME.
(I'm burning; stay away.)

K – · –
KILO
I HAVE SOMETHING TO
COMMUNICATE.
(I want to tell you something.)

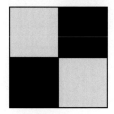

L · – · ·
LIMA
YOU SHOULD STOP
YOUR VESSEL.
(You need to stop your boat.)

M – –
MIKE
MY VESSEL IS STOPPED.
(I have stopped my boat.)

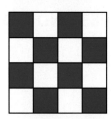

N – ·
NOVEMBER
NO!
(Negative)

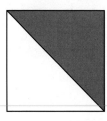

O – – –
OSCAR
MAN OVERBOARD.
(Someone fell off of the boat.)

When the shapes in two blocks
are the same,
the way the shapes are placed,
HORIZONTALLY or VERTICALLY,
gives a BLOCK a name, like "J" and "T."

P ·—— ·
PAPA
ALL ABOARD.
(People must
get on the boat.)

Blocks A, B, M, V and Z are the most DIFFICULT ones to make. Save them for AFTER you have practiced on lots of EASIER patchwork flags.

Block "I" is an appliqued patch. Page 38 shows you how.

Q ——·—
QUEBEC
I REQUEST FREE PRACTIQUE.
(I ask for customs clearance.)

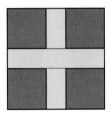

R ·—·
ROMEO
MY MOVEMENT IS RESTRICTED
BECAUSE THE WATER IS NOT
DEEP ENOUGH.

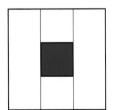

S ···
SIERRA
MY ENGINES ARE GOING FULL
SPEED ASTERN. (My boat is
moving backwards fast.)

T —
TANGO
KEEP CLEAR OF ME.
(Stay away.)

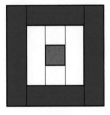

U ··—
UNIFORM
YOU ARE RUNNING INTO
DANGER. (You are moving
toward a bad area.)

V ···—
VICTOR
I REQUIRE ASSISTANCE.
(I need help.)

W ·——
WHISKEY
I REQUIRE MEDICAL ASSISTANCE.
(I need a doctor.)

X —··—
X-RAY
STOP CARRYING OUT YOUR
INTENTIONS.
(Don't do what you are doing.)

Y —·——
YANKEE
I AM DRAGGING MY ANCHOR.
(My anchor is in the water
behind my moving boat.)

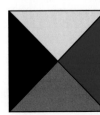

Z ——··
ZULU
I REQUIRE A TUG.
(I need someone to push me.)

red   yellow   black   blue   white

31

MAKE PATCHWORK ALPHABET BLOCK TEMPLATES

FOLLOW THE INSTRUCTIONS FOR TEMPLATE MAKING ON THE PATTERN SHEETS.

NOTE: Extra patterns may be ordered from Palmer/Pletsch at 1-800-728-3784.

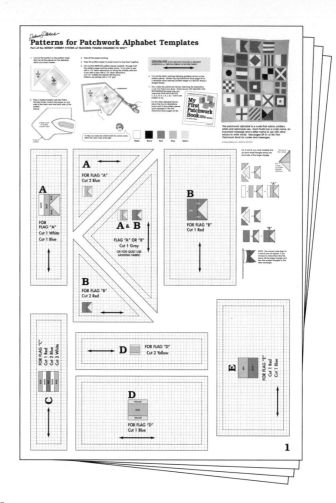

MAKE BLOCKS WITH SQUARES AND RECTANGLES the same way you made the FOUR PATCH BLOCK.

C, D, E, G, H, J, K, L, Q, T and **U** are EASIEST to do.
R and **X** are simple, too:

"R"

"X"

P and S both use the same shapes.

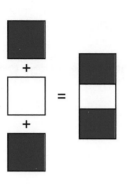 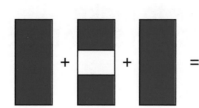  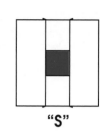

"P"   "S"

The center of **W** is a BLOCK like a small "S" (except for color).

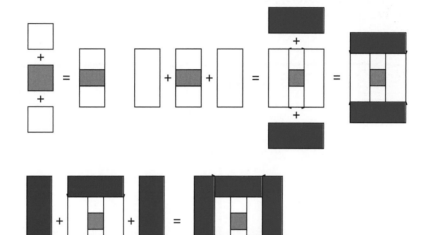

"W"

N uses 16 squares made using a 3½" SQUARE TEMPLATE.

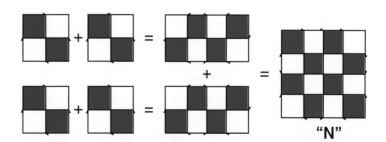

make four of these

"N"

MAKE PATCHWORK BLOCKS WITH TRIANGLES
when you KNOW how to make
PATCHWORK BLOCKS with SQUARES and RECTANGLES

BIAS EDGES STRETCH.

BIAS is the stretchy, diagonal line
in woven fabric.

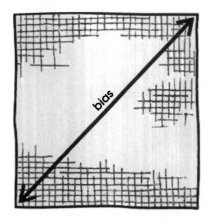

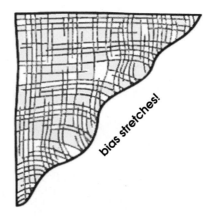

Use an IRON and SPRAY STARCH to stiffen fabric
to keep bias edges from stretching
before drawing, cutting and stitching.

PLACE THE OUTSIDE EDGES OF A BLOCK ON A STRAIGHT THREAD

The OUTSIDE edges of a BLOCK should NOT be bias.
Cut the fabric pieces so the OUTSIDE edges of the block are on a STRAIGHT THREAD.

To make **F** and **O** place the
TWO SHORT EDGES of the template
that make the SQUARE CORNER
on STRAIGHT THREADS.

To make **Z** and **V** and **M**
place the LONG EDGE
of the triangle TEMPLATE
on a STRAIGHT THREAD.

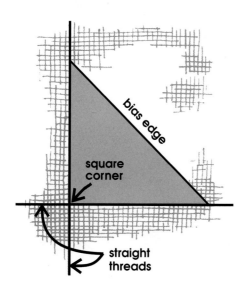

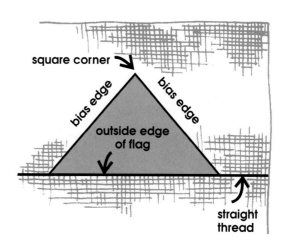

SEW BLOCKS WITH TRIANGLES

O and **Z** are the easiest blocks with triangles.

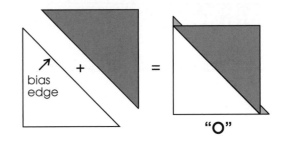

"O"

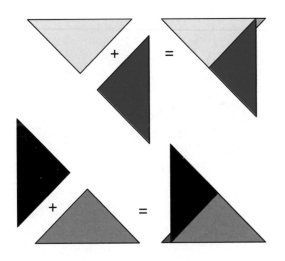

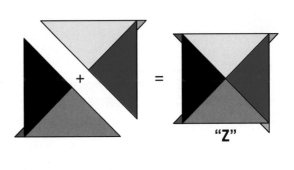

"Z"

M and **V** are a combination of triangles and strips.

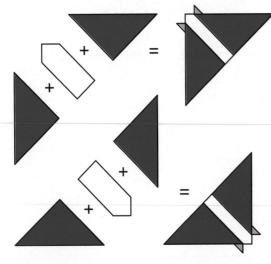

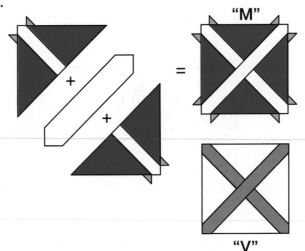

"M"

"V"

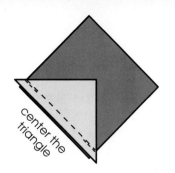

center the triangle

ATTACH TRIANGLES TO RECTANGLES AND SQUARES

The long edges of the triangles are LONGER than the sides of the squares. CENTER the triangles CAREFULLY.

For **F** by attach diagonal bias edges to the straight sides of a square.

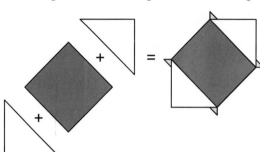

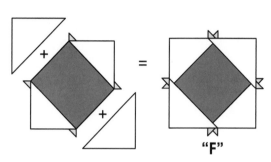

"F"

A uses two rectangles and three triangles.

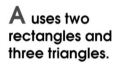

line up at this corner

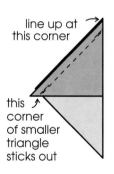

this corner of smaller triangle sticks out

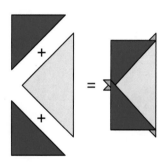

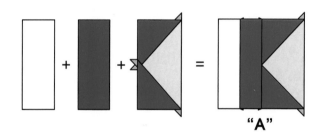

"A"

B uses one rectangle and three triangles.

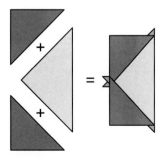

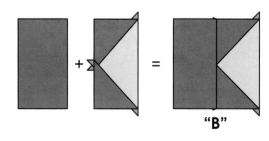

"B"

MAKE BLOCKS WITH STRIPS

Y has eight strips and a triangle at two corners. Cut the long edges of the strips along a straight thread.

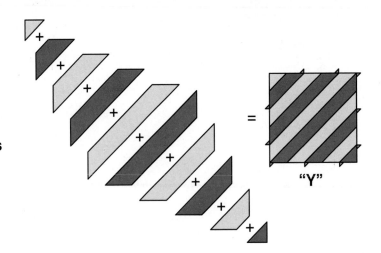

"Y"

MAKE AN APPLIQUÉ FLAG

Make "I" by APPLIQUÉING a circle on a square. Stitch by hand or by machine.

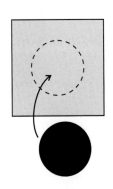

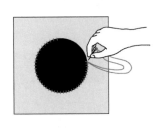

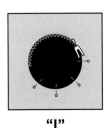

"I"

An APPLIQUÉ is a fabric shape stitched on TOP of a background.

If your sewing machine makes a ZIGZAG (SATIN) STITCH use it to attach the circle patch to the background square.

FINISH THE CODE FLAG BLOCKS

These blocks can be finished as a pillow, a flag, a framed picture, or made into a quilt as in the photo on the inside back cover of this book.

(A flag is made like a pillow
but without the stuffing.
Page 28 tells how.)

MAKE TEMPLATES FOR THE FOUR PATCH BLOCK

A TEMPLATE IS A PATTERN FOR PATCHWORK PATCHES.

1. Place a SQUARE CORNER of clear template plastic or poster board on top of a SQUARE CORNER on the TEMPLATE drawing on page 7.

2. TRACE the TEMPLATE. Use a pencil and a T-square or ruler to make STRAIGHT lines and SQUARE CORNERS.

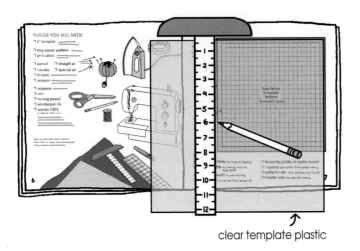

clear template plastic

To make TEMPLATES for the PATCHWORK ALPHABET BLOCKS, see page 32.

3. Cut out the TEMPLATE.
   (Use your paper scissors, not your good fabric scissors!)

Keep all the TEMPLATES for ONE BLOCK in ONE envelope or plastic bag, labeled with the BLOCK'S NAME.